No One Left to Hate

Cleveland Pimpton

*To: Ann Williams
A true friend
Rev. Cleveland Pimpton*

NO ONE LEFT TO HATE
BY Cleveland Pimpton

Copyright 2013 © Cleveland Pimpton
All rights reserved.

No part of this publication may be reproduced or transmitted in any form or by any means, electronic or mechanical, including photocopy, recording, or any information storage and retrieval system, without permission in writing from the publisher.

Requests for permission to make copies of any part of the work should be mailed to:

Authorship Publishing, LLC
ATTENTION: Permissions Department
6169 Lazy River Circle, Suite C
Dallas, TX 75241

Printed in the United States of America
BY
Authorship Publishing, LLC
Dallas, TX

I dedicate the writing of this book to the love of my life, my wife, Barbara W. Pimpton. She has stood by my side, loved, and encouraged me for forty years now. She is my rock. And to my children, Tanisha and Demond, you two have made the word "Daddy" the greatest word in the English language.

No One Left to Hate

Chapter 1 Planning a Future *1*

Chapter 2 Service to One's Country *4*

Chapter 3 A Heritage to Uphold *22*

Chapter 4 What About Tomorrow *48*

Chapter 5 Preacher, Let's Talk *56*

Chapter 6 Life's Decisions *68*

Chapter 7 News from the Past *81*

Chapter 8 Love is An Action Word *92*

Chapter 9 A Tested Friendship *103*

Cleveland Pimpton   *Planning A Future*

Chapter 1

Planning A Future

Here it is December 1963, and Thomas J. Hanger finds himself sitting at his desk trying to study for a final exam but there are too many other things on his mind.

One more semester to go, and in May, I'll graduate from Central State University and be commissioned into the U.S. Army as 1st Lieutenant Thomas J. Hanger, he thinks to himself. He understands there is a one hundred percent chance he'll be on his way to Vietnam, but he will be proud to serve his country anyway he can.

But before he goes off to fight in a foreign land, he plans to ask the girl of his dreams for her hand in marriage. He reaches into his desk drawer and takes out the engagement ring he plans to give her on their date this coming weekend. He admires it and smiles brightly to himself. He catches himself before he stares too long; right now, he's got to concentrate on this test. Physics is one of his required classes. He has no idea where he will ever use it, but so far, it has been one of his toughest classes. When this class is over, the only thing he will know for sure is how to spell physics. Why does a government major need physics? he asks himself.

As he heads down the hallway towards his physics class, someone tenderly touches his arm. "Hi handsome," a voice says. He looks at her and its Helen, the girl with whom he wants to have a life. As he looks into her sparkling blue eyes and sees that beautiful smile, he almost forgets about the horror of this one class. Thomas thinks to himself; this girl is a combination of both beauty and brains.

"I thought blonds weren't supposed to be smart?" he asked her.

"Well, I was smart enough to pick you. What does that say? Anyway, you know more than you think you do. Let's go ace this test, so we can head home," she tells him.

"You got it, beautiful, I'm ready."

The semester soon ends, and the grades are good. It's time for Thomas and Helen to head back to their hometown about 40 miles away. He is driving an old car, but it's dependable and runs well. It is a 1957 Chevy Bellaire. It's a hand-me-down family car that was passed to him from his dad when he got his driver's license. It's a true classic and he really enjoys cruising around in it.

As they pass through town, they see the Civil Rights marchers protesting in front of some local businesses. "Why do they stir up trouble? Everything is fine just the way it is. I hate them for stirring things up," says Thomas.

Helen replies, "You know you don't hate anyone and they just want to be treated fairly. If they want to go to Central State, I'm all for it."

Thomas looks at her and says, "You're so soft hearted. I bet you would be."

Chapter 2

Service to One's Country

It is finally here, May 1964, and Malcolm Echols graduates from Paul Lawrence Dunbar High School. As he looks out into the audience and spots Shirley, his girlfriend, he thinks to himself, once I graduate and get a job, I'm going to ask her to be my wife.

He tells his girlfriend, Shirley, he's going to junior college to study Air Conditioning and Refrigeration. "I'll work for a big company for two or three years, then I'll branch out on my own. One day, you'll look up and see trucks with *Echols's Air Conditioning and Refrigeration* on them. Then I'll be able to build you a house over in The Heights."

Shirley takes hold of his arm and tells him, "I don't need a house in The Heights to be happy, a home on Grand Street with a yard and a picket fence with you is all I need. Plus, there's nobody in The Heights that looks like us. If I'm going to have neighbors, I at least want them to speak."

The Heights is an all-white neighborhood where many doctors, lawyers, and wealthy business owners have built their homes. It is also a white-only neighborhood. It has been a running joke in the black community that one day when they make it big they're going to move to The Heights. As of right now, the only blacks you see are either working in the yards or cleaning homes. No one has ever formally said blacks couldn't live there, but no blacks can afford to live in The Heights. Although there is an unspoken rule that you have your place in the community, and it's best to stay in your place, everyone seems to have that dream of one day being able to afford to live in the nicest neighborhood in town.

A young girl like Shirley Wilson has a good understanding of how the world works, and being able to afford to live in the area and having the acceptance of those already there, are two different things. She understands that change will come very slowly in certain areas, and she doesn't really see herself as a trailblazer.

Shirley is very soft spoken, but possesses a very powerful voice. A voice so dynamic that when she sings, Malcolm believes the angels in Heaven stand and smile. Her singing style is a combination of both Mahalia Jackson and Aretha Franklin. Malcolm once asked her whom would she get to sing at their wedding when she was the best, and she simply replied that when the time came, they would figure that one out. Shirley loved to sing in the church choir, and *God's Amazing Grace* was one of her favorites, and Malcolm and most everyone else loved hearing her sing that song. Her voice causes her parents to shed tears of joy when she sings.

Tonight is graduation and there are a couple of parties where they want to go. Permission from their parents was given, so off they go into the night.

It is now summer and Malcolm has just graduated from high school. He gets a summer job at the local grocery store until it's time for him to leave for school. He wants to save money, and he has something that he would like to purchase by summer's end,

Cleveland Pimpton   *Service to One's Country*

a ring for her Shirley's finger. One day, as Malcolm gets in from his job at Allied Grocery, his mother tells him he has a letter from the Army on the coffee table in the living room. Malcolm looks at it and thinks, well, it's not like I thought it would be, but here is my draft notice. It was a plain white envelope with a United States heading on it, the letter inside said, *"Greetings; you are being inducted into the United States Army. You are to report to your local draft board on July 23, 1964."* After seeing those words, the rest sort of ran together. He places the letter back on the coffee table and goes in search of his mother.

    When he walks into the kitchen where his mother is sitting, he looks at her, and she has tears in her eyes. She tells him, "I know you have to serve your country, but with this war, I just don't understand what it is we're supposed to be fighting for."

    He gives her a big hug, "Mama; it's going to be alright, besides, didn't you tell me God is everywhere?"

"Your daddy is pulling a double shift at the plant, so sit down and eat your supper."

"Mama, as soon as I'm finished, I need to go over and give Shirley the news."

As he sits down to eat his meal, Malcolm reasons that nobody is happy about being drafted, but it wasn't unexpected. He will just have to factor two more years into his plans, but then he will have the G.I. Bill to help pay for college.

As he walks into the Wilson's house, he speaks as he has always done, but this time, there was something in his voice that told Mrs. Wilson that things were about to change. She calls to Shirley letting her know that Malcolm was there. Shirley comes to the door and instantly sees that something is wrong with the look on his face. She suggests that they go outside on the porch to talk. As he and Shirley sit on the front porch, he tells her that he has some bad news, and slowly he passes her the draft notice. Inside Shirley is crying, but she fights hard not to let it show on the outside. She sees that this news has devastated Malcolm, so she must stay strong for him. They both know several guys from the neighborhood who have also received their notices, so it wasn't a complete surprise.

So far, Malcolm has worked long hours and saved his money, so he could afford an engagement ring for Shirley. He wishes to give her something to let her know he wants to spend the rest of his life with her. The ring has been on lay-a-way at the jewelry store downtown. It was nearing the time for him to report for duty, and although they had both talked about and planned to complete college before they got married, he now wanted to give her the ring so she would have no doubt about how he really felt.

The night before Malcolm was to report to his induction site, he asked Shirley to marry him and to his surprise, she said "No, but I will wait for you. I want our wedding day to be special. When you get back from overseas, we'll have a nice church wedding." Shirley knew that was not the answer that he expected, but she did promise to wear it every day until he comes home. The ring is small, but she loves it just the same.

Malcolm walks through the large swinging doors of the bus terminal. There waiting for him was a bus full of other inductees. Some are trying to look brave and others with tears in their eyes, but all were headed for the same Army Boot Camp. He's off to serve his country.

ଔ ଓ

His training is tough and challenging, but Thomas survived and finally, it's graduation and commission day. It's a sunny humid day, which is typical for southern summers. 1st Lieutenant Thomas J. Hanger stands ready to receive his bars, but he also has other things on his mind as well. In two weeks, it will be 1st Lieutenant and Mrs. Thomas J. Hanger. That has a good ring to it, he thinks. He wonders if Helen will go along with him wanting to be married in his army uniform. Even so, hey, let's get this part of the day over with, after all, there are two graduations. Helen is graduating also and getting her nursing license and already has a job at the hospital back home. He hopes that will keep her mind occupied while I'm overseas.

Thomas and Helen stand before the minister in the church where they grew up. She is in her white flowing wedding gown, and he is in his army dress uniform. They have just enough time for a one-week honeymoon before he leaves. He already knows he will be looking forward to her letters to come in the mail. He feels so blessed because God made this one, especially for him to love.

When Lieutenant Hanger reports to his new duty station in Saigon, he stands before his commander, Col. Courtney. The Colonel tells him, "I see you graduated from my Alma Mata, Central State University. You know that means I have to make sure you are in good hands. I'm assigning you to a unit where I have some of my best men. Your non-com is a Sergeant Echols. Son, if you want to learn the ropes and make it back home alive, do whatever Sergeant Echols tells you. He can smell Charlie three clicks away, and all of his promotions have been field grade because he is that good."

To Hanger's dismay, Sergeant Echols is a young black kid who is younger than he is. After introductions are made, and Sergeant Echols shows him around and helps him get settled in, he thinks to himself, Col. Courtney wants me to take orders from this black guy who is not as old as I am. What has this Army come to?

As they prepare for their first night patrol, Sergeant Echols tells Hanger to take off all his ribbons and bars.

"I'm your commanding officer," he tells Echols.

"Sir, everybody knows that," Echols says.

"If you wear all that into the jungle, so will Charlie. The Viet Cong know a lot more about us than we know about them. This is their territory, so there is a really good chance they have eyes on us from the moment we leave camp. For all we know, some of the workers in our camp could be Charlie and reporting to their people on everything from manpower to the amount of food we have on hand. These sweeps last two to three days and we don't want to broadcast who our officers are because that could mean putting a target on your back, and I don't want to get a reputation of not being able to take care of my officers. I want to get you back to base in one piece."

Lieutenant Hanger agrees and does as Echols has instructed him to do. As time goes on and when they would venture out into the night on these patrols, Lieutenant Hanger not only came to depend on Sergeant Echols, he began to look up to this young black man. He was so impressed with him that it spilled over into his letters that he would write home to Helen. He tells her of Echol's heroic efforts and strategies that have let to successes on the battlefield. "Respect is something that a soldier earns from his fellow soldiers and there isn't a man in their unit who doesn't look up to Echols. I hate these Viet Cong, and I look forward to when my time over here is up, so I can get back home to you."

As always, Helen writes back. It was in her latest reply that she writes with important news. "You know you don't hate anyone. They are fighting for their country just like you're fighting for yours. Now please be careful, the baby and I will be waiting for you when you come home." This was her way of letting him know she was expecting. He read those lines over and over again, and then he looked at the envelope to make sure this letter was addressed to him. The address does say Lieutenant Thomas J. Hanger, and that's him. He smiles to himself and beams with pride. He just knows it's going to be a boy.

A yell is heard all over the camp as Hanger goes throughout the camp showing the letter to everybody. "Hey man, I'm going to be a father," he tells everyone, and he can't wait to find Sergeant Echols. When he sees him, he tells him, "Sergeant, man, help me make it out of here. I have a baby boy waiting on me back in the states."

Cleveland Pimpton *Service to One's Country*

    This man has become more than just a sergeant. He's become a friend. Hanger grew up never giving a real thought about black people. Things were the way they were and that was that, but this Sergeant Echols is the greatest thing since sliced bread. Their friendship has developed into more than just two guys from the same state. Hanger doesn't see Echols as this black guy who takes orders from him, but as a true friend who is as concerned about his welfare as much as his own. When you eat, sleep, and fight together a bond develops between two men that transcend color. Whenever they have some down time, he loves to hear Echols talk about the girl with the golden voice and their plans for the future. While other guys are getting Dear John letters from their wives and girlfriends back home, these two guys know the women in their lives will always stand behind them.

    Hanger comes to understand that regardless of color, every man over here who is fighting for his country deserves the best America has to offer when they get back to the states. He now feels that the color of one's skin doesn't keep you from dying or help you live any longer. He never saw this day coming, but he is starting to agree with Helen that every American deserves America's best, and he would walk beside Echols whether in the jungle or down a city street.

When their rotation comes up to go on a night patrol one night, Hanger detects a strange feeling in his gut. Before heading out, he tells Echols, "Sergeant keep your head up. This one is more than just routine." As they are making their way through the jungle and just as daybreak comes, an all-out assault by Charlie. Hanger is well-seasoned by now, and he does not need anybody to hold his hand. He's heard barking out orders to his men as they return fire.

Suddenly, he sees Charlie coming straight toward him with the look of fire in his eyes. Hanger raises his weapon, an M-16, and fires two quick bursts, and Charlie drops within ten feet of him. Just like that, the firefight is over. They received a few scratches, but all of his guys are all right. They do a body count check and as Hanger looks over the dead body of the Charlie he killed, it hits him, this is his first confirmed kill. He can't feel overjoyed. The guy looks to be about twenty years old, and he had no choice but to take his life. Where is the joy in that?

Helen's words from his last letter rang in his ears. "You know you don't hate anybody, but war is all about killing." Hanger carries the letter from Helen in his shirt pocket and reads it every chance he gets. It has become his reason for living. However, at the moment, the most important thing is getting to base camp, and the one man he knows he can depend on is Sergeant Echols. "Let's get 'em back Sergeant; it's time for a little R&R." He's starting to sound like a real war veteran.

Back at camp, the atmosphere is calmer and everyone feels as if they can act as normal and let their guard down. Someone is always on the perimeter walking and patrolling the area. But one late night, there is an attack on the camp. Everyone falls out of his bunk and scrambles to his assigned foxhole and starts to return fire in the direction where they see muzzle flashes in the jungle. Out of nowhere, a grenade drops at the foot of Lieutenant Hanger. As both Hanger and Echols look at each other, there is no time to think. Echols instinctively knows that it's his responsibility to take care of his brother-in-arms. Suddenly, he jumps over and covers the grenade with his body, and as it explodes Hanger is hit in the leg by some shrapnel, but he really doesn't feel a thing. The only thing he can feel right now is his heart about to jump out of his chest.

He grabs Echols and calls for a Medic. He's shouting for help and praying all at the same time as he is holding Echols for what seems to be an eternity. While waiting on help to arrive, Sergeant Echols asks him for a favor, "There's a letter in my top pocket from Shirley. Would you please read it to me? I read it once, but I want to hear what it says one more time. You see Lieutenant, I'm going to be a father too. Man, you should hear her sing. When she stands to sing *God's Amazing Grace,* the angels in Heaven stand at attention. A beautiful mom with a great voice, I wish I were going to be around to see him." Hanger opens the letter with blood-stained fingers. He scans the letter for those important words from home. He starts to read the part where Shirley is telling Malcolm he's going to be a father. As Sergeant Malcolm hears the words, he smiles and quietly goes to sleep.

Hanger is lost in his thoughts; this really can't be happening. Echols had only thirty days left on his tour, and he's going to be a father just like me. He hollers for help, but it's already too late. The man he has come to respect and have true brotherly love for has unselfishly given his own life to save his. How can a debt of this magnitude ever be repaid? I'll never be able to face his family, how do you thank a parent when they will never hear the voice of their son again? How do you tell a child you don't have your father because of me?

The body of Sergeant Echols was put in a body bag, and all his belongings are boxed up to be returned to state side. When Malcolm's body arrives on American soil, his family is gathered at the local funeral home to view his body. His mother and father prepare to say farewell to their son as Shirley Wilson sits with the family holding her and Malcolm's child. With tears in her eyes, she realizes the child she is holding will never know its father. Raising this child will be her job and hers alone; but strangely enough, after the funeral Shirley had lost her desire and her voice to sing. The only time she could sing was when she rocked baby Malcolm.

There had not been a military funeral at their church since the Korean War. The people gathered until every pew in the church was full. Then they stood around the walls and outside on the churchyard. Everyone from the elderly to Malcolm's high school classmates was there. Some even wore their military uniforms in his honor because they were headed overseas to do their part in serving their country. A couple of city officials made an appearance. This was by far the largest military funeral this town had ever seen, but unfortunately, it would not be the last. Vietnam would take a toll on this city the same as it would on every town, both large and small, across America. When families in other communities received word of their son dying in combat, they could depend on Mr. and Mrs. Echols to be there to comfort them. Even though it revived the pain of losing their son, they felt it was their duty to help those who were also dealing with such a great loss.

Chapter 3

Heritage to Uphold

Charles W. Walker III was a young man with a rich heritage. His grandfather, Charles W. Walker Sr. was a descendent of slaves who worked and lived on plantations in Louisiana and Texas. When word reached Texas of the Emancipation Proclamation, his ancestors moved from the plantation to the hill country of Texas. Charles Sr. was the first in his family to be born a free black man. That pride carried over to him being the first to graduate from high school and to serve his country in the United States Army during World War I. While serving his country, he distinguished himself in combat and received several medals, only to return home to a hero's welcome and then be told to stay in his place. He understood what that meant, but he also knew, deep down, that what he had fought for was a better day for his children and grandchildren.

Charles W. Walker Jr. was a young man who had graduated from high school and was well into his first year of college when America was pulled into World War II with the bombing of Pearl Harbor. When his draft notice arrived, he had no issue with reporting for duty to serve his country. His father had drilled it into him that it was an honor to fight for your country. Charles Jr. applied for and was accepted into the Tuskegee Pilot Training Program for blacks. Once they were allowed into battle, all noticed his phenomenal skills as a fighter pilot. He and his squad never lost a bomber while escorting them into the theater of war, and by the time the war was over Charles had earned the title of "Ace."

Once he returned home from the war, he displayed his medals on the wall of their den in a shadow box right next to his fathers. He had proudly served his country, came home to a hero's welcome, and was told to stay in his place. He was allowed to fight for his country, but not permitted to vote. That right was still reserved for whites only, but like his father, he knew he had fought for a better day for his children. Some changes had taken place, but there was still a long way to go. In spite of it all, he went on to graduate from Tuskegee Institute and to become a successful businessman within the black community.

Charles W. Walker III was in college at the beginning of the civil rights struggle. He wanted to stand up and march in Montgomery with Dr. King, but his dad advised him to think about what he was trying to accomplish in college. "Don't do anything that will hamper your being commissioned as an officer in the Army," he told him. "Your presence there as an officer will be just as important as those who march through the streets". Therefore, he listened to his father and poured all of his energy into finishing college. Upon graduation from college, Lieutenant Charles W. Walker III received his commission and immediately reported to his duty station in Virginia for training.

There were also other plans for the future he had in his mind. During his junior year of college, he met the most gorgeous girl in the world, Claire Anderson. She would stroll across the campus as if she owned the place. When Charles saw her, he knew some things would have to change, and if he were lucky, it would start with her last name. For him, it was love at first sight, and each day they spent getting to know one another made him that much more determined that they would grow old together.

Claire didn't tell him at the time, but from the moment they laid eyes on each other she knew her mother was right. "Honey, when you meet him, you will know. Nobody will have to tell you that's the man for you. God will tell your heart, and the rest will take care of itself," she always said. So she too knew that they would grow old together.

They spent countless hours talking about their future together, and their plans were made. He would be an officer in the Army, and she would become a teacher at the local school. After all, military kids would need a teacher who could relate to them.

The wedding was set to happen during the period after his officer training was complete, and before he was to report to his new duty station. Claire was by far the most beautiful bride to walk down the aisle. Charles stood there in his dress blue uniform waiting to say I do. Their families had gathered at the historic Bethany Baptist Church of Atlanta where Claire's family was some of the founding members after slavery.

Their mothers seemed to have formed a bond even before they were tied together by marriage. They loved shopping and sipping hot tea in the afternoons. Their dads also got along well. They enjoyed chatting together about the rich heritage of each family, and they both had shops out back of their homes where they would tinker and build things. This was also the place where they could have a little nip without being fussed at by the women.

After the wedding, the only thing Charles wasn't looking forward to were those assignments where Claire wouldn't be allowed to go with him. There would be those overseas assignments that would not allow the spouses to accompany their soldiers. If they ever felt there were too many of those tours that kept them apart, they would have to adjust their plans. He thought that if he did not stay the full twenty, whatever time he spent in the military would be an asset to his career goals.

The first year of the marriage was good. Charles was assigned to a base in Washington state. He was one of only a few black officers on the post. Charles won the respect of several ranking officers, and he could easily flow between commanding troops in the field and those mandatory black tie events. With Claire on his arm, they never missed a step.

One Friday after releasing his troops for the weekend Charles arrived home to find Claire had fixed his favorite meal with all the trimmings. After he finished the beef tips and noodles, he sat in his recliner in the den waiting for her to tell him how much money she had saved him on whatever she had bought. Instead, she sat on the arm of the chair and presented him with a cigar with a blue wrapper on it saying, "It's a boy." They spent the rest of the weekend on the phone talking to family, sharing the good news.

Charles dreamed of all the things he would be able to do with his son and all the lessons he wanted to teach him. Claire knew the name was automatic, Mr. Charles W. Walker IV. Even if she wanted a different first name, she wouldn't dare to mention it and hurt her husband's feelings. Claire understood to come from people whose heritage had been erased through slavery to where they are today, was very important to both families. That is why she was shocked to hear Charles tell her father that he thought the baby's name should be Charles Anderson Walker. Anderson was Claire's maiden name and a proud name that would honor both families. It made her dad happy and even his dad approved of the idea.

Charles reported to the base at 7:00 a.m. Monday morning with the good news, only to be greeted by news from the base commander. At the beginning of the staff meeting, Charles and several other men received promotions, and Charles was given his 1st Lieutenant's bars. Then came the news that had been rumored for months. Word has come down from the Pentagon that the United States military troop presence in Vietnam was about to take a big jump. Over half the troops stationed on their base are receiving orders for combat duty there. The unit Lieutenant Walker commanded would be shipped out in ninety days. They knew this could come, and they've talked about it and prepared for it, but now that it's really here it's still a shock.

    Charles decided to wait until he got home to give Claire the news. He did not want to tell her something like this over the phone. Little did he know, the word had spread all over the base and into town. By the time he arrives home, Claire greets him at the door with tears in her eyes. Once the quietness of the evening settles in some decisions needed to be made. Claire cannot stay in Washington by herself. They call her family and talk with them and it is decided that Claire will go back to Atlanta and stay with her family so she will not be alone during her pregnancy. Having her mother and sisters around will keep her from worrying about him off in some foreign jungle.

His priority is the safety and well-being of Claire and the baby. Within a couple of weeks, their house is packed up, and everything will be put in storage in Atlanta. They will make a stop in Texas to visit his family for a few days and then go on to Atlanta. Charles must be back in Washington for troop training in thirty days to prepare for deployment. With his family taken care of, he can concentrate on the combat training that will help him make it back home safely.

Within that ninety-day period, their training was complete and orders were cut for Vietnam. Upon arrival in Da Nang, Lieutenant Walker led his troops off the transport plane. As they walked down the flight line, the one thing that caught the eyes of everyone was the number of caskets lined up to for shipment back to the states for burial. Walker whispers a prayer, "Lord, I'm in your hands. Please return me back home to Claire in an upright position. I want to be a lot of things, but a husband and father are the most important." As they settled in, he noticed that things were the same over here in a war zone as in the United States. He is only one of a few black officers in command position.

Within a week of writing Claire, he receives a letter back from her telling him to be careful. Her mother and father are excited over the fact that their first grandchild will be born in the same hospital where she was born. They have a bedroom already fixed up for his folks when they come to visit. The two future grandmothers are planning things they will be able to do together when they come for the birth of the baby.

Knowing that his wife and baby are taken care of Charles can concentrate keeping his head out of Charlie's line of fire. The days become weeks and the weeks become months as they go about their routine patrol duties. The firefights become very intense and the loss of life has a tendency to dull your senses to the point of complete numbness. It has been six months, and he can't remember the number of letters he has had to write to the families of men who had proudly served under his command. The one thing that keeps him sane are the letters and pictures he receives from Claire. He can see her progress with the pregnancy from the pictures and wishes he could be there to touch her stomach and feel the baby move. Never in a million years did he ever think he would miss the birth of their first child, but he will be about three and a half to four months old when he sees him for the first time. Between the taking of life and missing the birth of his son, he wonders if a career in the military is what he really wants.

Charles displayed his heroic character and leadership on the battlefield and for that, he was promoted to Captain. His unit was sent out on patrol, and they encountered another unit that had been pinned down by the enemy. One of the worst firefights that he has ever been in ensues, and two men were lost and several wounded, but they made it back to base. When Captain Walker reports to base camp, he is summoned to the commander's office. Once inside a military chaplain approaches him. Charles knows that it must be bad news, and so immediately he assumed it was about one of his parents, but when the chaplain told him the news, it was as though he had been hit in the chest with a fifty-pound sledge hammer.

While he was out on patrol, the news came that his wife, Claire, was involved in an auto accident. The injuries she sustained were so severe they caused her to go into premature labor. She died before they could get her to the hospital. Once Charles was able to get his breath his only question was about his baby. "Were they able to save my baby?" he asked. "How is my child?" he demanded. The look on their faces told the whole story.

"Sorry Captain, they weren't able to save either of them," says the Chaplin.

Colonel Bishop tells him his time left on his tour is so short that orders have already been cut to get him back to the states ASAP. The Red Cross says the family has taken care of everything, and will wait for him to get there for the funeral. Colonel Bishop tells Charles the mission he was on was too important to jeopardize by trying to get him out when they first got the word. The mission was more important than my wife and baby, Charles thinks to himself. "Maybe to you sir, but it was my wife and child. I wish someone had given me the option to make that call."

Bishop says, "I understand son, get your gear together, wheels up at 0500. I hate to lose you like this. You're a fine officer and deserve to return home to good news."

"Thank You Sir," Charles says with tears in his eyes.

On his way back to his unit, Charles can only think about how much he hates this war. I'm over here in a foreign country taking lives in the name of freedom and at the same time my wife and child are being taken away from me by some fool not paying attention to where he was going. When I find out whom it was that took my family from me, jail will be the safest place for them, he thinks to himself.

On the long flight back, Captain Walker can only think about how much he now hates the military for having him so far away from Claire and the baby when they needed him the most. As soon as my time is up, they can have this uniform and for all it stands. The life and career he once looked forward to is what has cheated him out of the most precious moments of his life. He is in a hurry to get back to a place he really doesn't want to be.

Charles arrives at the Atlanta Metro Airport and is greeted by his mom and dad, along with Claire's family. There are smiles and tears as he embraces each of them. He understands that he can't go to the funeral home at three in the morning, but he will be standing on the steps when they open so he can see Claire and their child for the first and maybe the last time. He's tired, but his eyes won't close, so as he watches the sunrise he can only think about all those letters he wrote to the families of men he had lost. Now he wonders if those words really made a difference. Nothing seems to dull the pain of losing the two people he loved the most.

It is now 8:30 a.m. as Charles walks through the doors of Frazier and Sons Funeral Home. He is directed to a room where there is a casket holding the bodies of Claire and baby Charles. It was a beautiful sight. The way they had the baby lying in her arms, a sight he had looked forward to seeing, but not like this. Although his family was there to support him, the pain of seeing them lying there was more than he could bear. All of his hopes and dreams for the future now lay in front of him awaiting burial in the cold ground. The love he has for them is the only thing that outweighs the hate he feels for the driver of the vehicle that took them from him. Now, the only thing he can do is say farewell to his love and hello to the feelings of hate towards all those responsible for having him so far away from his family when they needed him the most.

The next day at the funeral the sun shone beautifully as though Claire ordered it so everyone could feel the bright rays of her smile from Heaven as they said good-bye. Charles made it through the day, the same as he had done all those horrible days in Nam. The courage he had displayed in battle now helped him to stand strong for his loved ones. The minister spoke words of hope, love, and of God's grace. He heard all that was said and then again, not a word. He could not concentrate on the message. His emotions were vacillating between rage and despair. It was a hard day, but he made it through. Having to leave the two most precious gifts from God, left a hole in his soul that could never be filled.

Claire's family assured him he would always be a part of their family, but Charles knew from this day on every time he saw them, he would only be able to think of what could have been and all that had been taken away from him. How could they ever really want him around? He hated everything he was feeling right now, but he had to get things wrapped up so he could report to his new base and carry on as though nothing had happened. He hated the thought of moving on without Claire, but there is more at stake here than just his feelings. There is a heritage to uphold. What was really more important, love of family or love of country? His family had taught him there was no real separation there. Charles moved on to his new duty station while upholding the family tradition of proudly serving his country. Three generations of Walkers have now proudly served, but it ends with him since his son will not be able to do so.

Captain Walker was honorably discharged from the Army a few months later and starts his new life in the civilian world. He does not have anything good to say about the military after what he feels they did to him, but being a war hero sits well with potential employers as he searches for his new life without Claire and baby Charles. Austin, Texas is where he really wants to live since he does have family there, but there is something pulling him back to the Atlanta area. The potential job market is very good there, and he soon lands a position with Telco Communications Inc., which is a leader in the growing communications field. Using his business savvy he learned from his dad and the discipline he gained in the military, Charles is a rapid climber up through the corporate ranks. All the single women on the job consider him the perfect catch, but none were able to hook him. There is plenty of conversation around the water fountain about why he is so elusive. They've all taken their best shot at him, and nothing has paid off.

    Living in Atlanta, the one place you could count on finding Charles was at the cemetery where Claire and the baby were buried. Every Friday about 5:30 pm, he arrived there in his sleek black Mercedes. He would get out a blanket, and sit by their grave. Sometimes he would talk to them and drink, and other times he would just sit there and drink. When it gets too dark to read the headstone, he packs up and leaves. On this particular hot Friday in

July, Charles is sitting there when Claire's mom walks up. "Charles," she says, "you never come by the house, but I know where to find you every Friday. Son, we need to talk. My daughter loved you too much to want you to grieve yourself to death. She would want you to live the life God has given you."

"Living doesn't seem to be all it's cracked up to be," says Charles.

"Son, we miss Claire also and we're thankful to know she had found the love of her life," says Mrs. Anderson, "but it's been almost two years. We've accepted the fact God called her and the baby home to be with Him. We don't like it any more than you do, but we have to accept it. Bill and I have watched you come here and cry each Friday, hoping one day you would get it out of your system. Now we love you too much to let you die inside. Come follow me home now. We've got dinner on the table for you and someone with whom Bill and I think you need to talk. That's not a request. When I turn the corner I except to see you in my rearview mirror." He remembered Claire telling him that when her mother started talking like that she would not take no for an answer, so he made sure he followed her home.

As Charles pulled up to the Andersons home he remembered the last time he was there. Could he step inside? Mrs. Anderson took him by the arm. "It's hard for all of us," she told him.

It was good to see Mr. Anderson. Charles didn't realize just how much he had missed them. Now he was starting to feel guilty for not realizing their great loss. They sat and talked for about a half hour before the doorbell rang. It was Rev. Washington, the pastor who had performed his and Claire's wedding. He was also the one who had the sad duty to deliver her eulogy. Charles is now starting to think that must have been a sad day for him also. He had known Claire all her life and had baptized her when she was a young girl. Once they had gotten the small talk out of the way, he got straight to the point. "Charles, are you upset with God because of what he allowed to happen?" he asked.

Charles replied, "Upset is putting it mildly." Once he started talking, it all came flooding out. He was mad at God, hated the Army, and all those responsible for sending him away when they needed him the most.

Rev. Washington explained to him how love would always keep Claire alive in his heart, but the hate he was holding onto would slowly destroy that memory and never allow him to love again. "Love and hate can never reside in the same temple at the same time. Whichever one you feed the most will overcome the other. Charles, which one are you feeding?" he asked. "You have a reputation in town as a take no prisoner businessman. If there is a negotiation going on, I want you on my team. You can see the people on the other side of the table, but your heart seems to go blind when it comes to concessions. That's not the Charles I remember and certainly not the one Claire loved."

"Pastor, I put my life in the hands of the military because I was told to serve proudly and your country will take care of you," Charles tells him. "There were decisions made which were supposed to be in the best interest of the country, but never considered my family. I wasn't given a choice. So, who should I look out for now? I hate the very thought of love of my country. You go and kill in our name, but we decide whether or not you can be with your wife and baby when they need you the most. I'm just operating the way they taught me. It is not personal, just business."

"Charles, I would like for you to come to church this Sunday. I will be preaching on how to find real love. There are two things one must do in order to find love, forgive others, and most important, forgiveness of self. No one was really trying to hurt you when those decisions were made. You have to forgive yourself for not being there at a critical time. Life isn't always fair. If you promise me you'll be there Sunday, I'll leave you alone tonight."

Charles looks at him for what seems to be an eternity and finally says, "Alright, I'll see you Sunday." He thanks his in-laws for caring enough to want to see him live even though their daughter was dead.

He attended that Sunday service and then found himself going back the next Sunday without any prodding from the Andersons. The change that was taking place within him was noticeable by all on and off the job. Even those he negotiated against shook his hand when it was over. He found himself mentoring some of the younger men in church and teaching the young adult Sunday school class.

It had been evident to many, but seemed to come as a shock to himself when he realized God was calling him into the ministry. Charles had a natural love, compassion, and concern for the people of the church and no one was happier than his in-laws, the

Andersons. Even though Claire was no longer with them, there was a special kind of love they saw in Charles because of her. They always knew she had picked the right man. Now, here they all were, both families, gathered together again, in the same church where Charles and Claire were married. The same church they had to bid farewell to her and the baby, and now Charles is set to deliver his first sermon for the Lord. Charles thought to himself, if only Claire could be here to stand by me today.

His sermon topic was "Discovering Real Love," and he delivered it with the power and grace of a seasoned veteran of the pulpit. Pastor Washington was proud of his newest son in the ministry. Once the service was over Charles told him he now felt he was capable of moving forward. He had been able to forgive himself for not being there and understood that God really is in charge. He wants to go further in his mission with God, and so he has decided to attend the seminary. Pastor Washington tells him he will one day make a fine pastor because the hate he once carried around has now been replaced with love. "When your heart is full of love there is no one left to hate," he tells him, "especially yourself."

Charles divides his time between the office and the church. He goes out on dates from time to time, but can never reach the point of getting serious. His heart still belongs to Claire. Pastor Washington warns him not to try to replace Claire, but "allow yourself to love someone for who they are."

Mrs. Anderson had told him, "We always want you to remember Claire, but Son you deserve a life. Allow the right woman to have her place in your heart."

So, Charles goes about his business and waits for God to move. He has done well in the business community. His company has gone through several changes, as the communications world seems to change daily. As Vice President of the Wireless Network Division, Telco Communications has become a national leader in the field, and Charles highly sought after by other companies.

With changes taking place, internally and externally, Telco has to downsize to stay competitive. Everyone is shocked when Charles decides to accept a severance package and steps away from the business world. Some think he is going to set up his own wireless business and others are waiting to see for which of the competitors he will go to work. They have paid him well, and he has invested wisely, so he has enough to live on for years to come. In fact, looking at his portfolio, he is quite well off.

Everyone is surprised except Pastor Washington and his in-laws. Pastor Washington has recommended Charles for the position of Pastor at The First Baptist Church in Hallsville, his old friend there has decided to retire. The church has heard him preach; his interview went well, and he received word from Deacon Echols that they will be offering Charles the Pastorate next week.

Chapter 4

What About Tomorrow

It's late on a Thursday evening; Helen is sitting on the front porch of the small house they rented rocking baby Paul in her arms. Helen had been expecting to hear from Thomas about when he would be coming home. His last letter told her when he would be leaving Vietnam and the number of stops he would have to make on his way. Every evening after dinner, she and Paul would sit on the porch and rock while looking at every car that passed, hoping it would stop and let Thomas out. They would sit and watch the people go by. They would smile and wave at some and speak to others. She thought this day would be like all the others, but then a taxi stops in front of the house and Capt. Thomas J. Hanger steps out and with baby in arms, she almost jumped over the fence to welcome him home.

There is a big welcome home dinner for Thomas, but the center of attention is baby Paul. Hanger is so amazed and vows to

Helen he will make up for not being there when Paul was born and missing the first few months of his life. As the evening winds down, he tells Helen he plans to get out of the army when his time is up. He wants something different. The question is what to do with the rest of his life.

Thomas is lucky, he's able to finish up his tour of duty at the army base just a few miles away. Fighting in Vietnam has taken away his desire for a career in the military. There are job offers from car sales to the insurance business, but nothing that really stands out. However, with a wife and baby to support, he really needs to get his feet on the ground.

On a quiet evening at home with Helen and baby Paul, the sereneness of the day was broken by the sound of police sirens and squealing tires. As they step onto the front porch, they see two police cars have stopped a young kid, and the officers are dragging him out of a car that they later find out is stolen. In his mind, there was a lot of unnecessary hitting with clubs and kicking the kid while he was down. He may have been wrong, but was all that necessary.

As darkness approaches, the events of the evening weigh heavily on his mind. He can only think about how he would have handled that situation. Without telling Helen where he was going, he leaves home early the next morning headed for police headquarters.

Within a couple of weeks, he has his application completed and has even had one interview. He can now tell Helen what he wants to do with his life all the while assuring her that his safety would not be an issue. After all, didn't he make it through Vietnam. She tells him of all the trauma she's seen come through the emergency room. Knowing all along, his mind is already made up.

Thomas did not like the way he saw that young man treated that day. He knew better than to bring that up during his review board; some things can only be changed from within. In a few months, Army Capt. Thomas J. Hanger would become Police Officer T. J. Hanger.

The training at The Regional Police Academy is pretty much a breeze for Thomas compared to what he had gone through in the jungles of Nam. The only thing that was a bit unsettling was when they went to the firing range. The sound of gunfire would cause him mentally to revert to a place he really did not want to go. Sometimes when he fires his weapon, he can see that young kid running towards him and dropping a few feet away. The training sergeant, Joe Turnwell, is a sharp guy. Thomas was not the first vet who had come through the academy after being in combat. He could recognize the symptoms by watching their body language. In those instances, he would stop the firing and pull that individual off the firing line. Qualifying with a weapon was not a problem for a military veteran. Keeping your head in the present is the important thing. On the streets, your life or your partner's life could depend on where your head is. You have to make sure you keep your head in the game. Thomas was surprised to realize he had not been able to shake the trials of war off as easily as he had thought. However, with the help of Sergeant Turnwell, and talking with guys who had come ahead of him, he was able to get his feet planted firmly on the ground.

Some even questioned him about why he wanted to be a cop when he was already a college graduate. All the cadets called him Joe College. Being a cop was considered a blue-collar job. There were questions about his choice of career that even he couldn't answer. He just knew it was the right choice for him, and this was where he belonged.

Moving up through the ranks was fairly easy, with two years in each rank, and you are eligible to test for the next step. Every two years Thomas was topping the promotion list. Helen was really happy when he made supervisor because that got him off the streets and out of harm's way. It did not matter what he said she could not help but worry. After all, this was the man she loved. Helen did give him one piece of advice that turned out to be very valuable. She told him, "If you are determined to make this your life's work, then you need to go back to college and get a Master's Degree. Everything is changing, and education is going to be what those choosing the leaders of the future are going to be looking for. Everybody wants the best, so then they will not have to look far. The right man will be right there under their noses." Remembering how smart she was, he took her advice, and by the time he made lieutenant, he had received his Master's Degree in Public Administration with a minor in Law Enforcement.

    The chief recognized Thomas' potential and made good use of it. There were new inventions in technology coming out on a daily basis it seemed, and the one man who seemed to understand how to integrate this new technology into the department was Thomas Hanger. With his knowledge of technology and his command skills, everybody within the department and some members of the city council considered Thomas Hanger a perfect fit to become the next Chief of Police. Thomas certainly did the work, but he knew the one responsibility for his rise to power was Helen Hanger. She was his most valuable advisor. He said it himself many years ago when they were in college, "Beauty and brains, what a combination." Even though she didn't necessarily agree with his decision to become a police officer, she always trusted his instincts. Now it appears, he is poised to become the next chief. Chief Reynolds called him in recently for a private conversation. He informed Thomas he was planning to retire at the end of the year. At the next city council meeting, he will notify them he is appointing Thomas to become his new Chief of Detectives. This move will officially make him second in command of the department. If the City Council is smart, there should not be any problem with appointing him as Chief. "They will get used to seeing you here by my side at all the council meetings and when it comes to budgetary and other issues involved in the running of the department, you will be the man making those presentations. They have to get used to dealing with you, so they can become comfortable with you. Thomas, I'm not just hand picking you for this job. This department has been my life, and if I have ever seen a man who is qualified and ready to assume command, it's you. This department will grow and prosper under your leadership, so I know I'm leaving it in good hands."

Later in the year, Thomas is before the council to present the department's budget for the upcoming year. Once they vote to approve, the Mayor asked him to stay for a moment. He starts talking about Chief Reynolds' retirement, having the right man for the job, and making a smooth transition in the leadership of the department. The Mayor then makes a motion and calls for a vote to appoint Thomas Hanger as Chief of Police starting at the beginning of the new year.

Chapter 5

Preacher, Let's Talk

In a small town, about 50 miles from Centerville, a little boy is taking his first steps. This is a joyous occasion to say the least. As his mother Shirley stands behind him holding his hands, the man encouraging him to com'on, and takes that first step is his grandfather. As little Malcolm takes those first steps Mr. Echols can't help but think about his son taking his first steps in this same room. As little Malcolm moves his feet forward, Mr. Echols tell Shirley, "Now he's ready to take on the world! Do you and the baby need anything?" he asked her. "You know we will always be here for you." He says, as he wishes his son had lived to see his fine baby boy.

"No we're fine," replied Shirley, "you and Mother Echols watching him while I'm in class is a big help. In a few months, I will have my nursing degree. Then we won't be such a burden on you and my folks."

"No such thing as a burden dear," says Mr. Echols, "when you love someone it's not a burden; it's a blessing. Now you two go head and get home before the sun catches you."

With no help from the government, because she and Malcolm were not married when little Malcolm was born, it's been a tough go financially. However, they are making it. The Echols gave her a major portion of the insurance money from the military. They told her it was for their grandchild. Out of everything she has had to deal with, telling her folks she was pregnant was probably the toughest. Without Malcolm by her side, her folks went with her to tell the Echols.

Instead of throwing her out, they embraced and prayed with her. "Honey, we know how much our son loves you," Mrs. Echols told her. "He even showed me the ring he wanted to give you before he left going to Vietnam." At that point, Shirley reaches into her purse and pulls the ring out. She can now proudly wear this ring. It will suffice until God says differently..

A few months later as Shirley pushes baby Malcolm down the street in his stroller, she thinks to herself, even when you make a mistake, God still shows his love for us. Now it is up to me to make all this work and give my baby a good home.

With the help of his grandparents, little Malcolm grows up into a fine young man. He never really asked for a lot because he knows Mama is trying to do everything on her own. She teaches him that if you want something in life, get up and go to work. This work ethic is enforced by his grandfathers. If he wants to make some money, they find something for him to do by helping them. The one he spends the most time with him gets bragging rights for the week.

His grandmothers, on the other hand, will spoil him rotten if given the chance. According to Malcolm, he has a pretty good life. That is, pretty good except for on Sundays. He has to go to Sunday school and 11:00 a.m. service. He does not really mind, but sometimes the preacher is really boring. He gets along well with other kids too. The entire community knows his story. When they have those special father and son days, one of his grandfathers is always with him. None of the other kids ever asked where his father was.

The pastor of their church decided to retire. Thank God, no more boring sermons, Malcolm thinks to himself. The search committee goes into action looking for his replacement. After a couple of months of hearing all those different preachers, the entire church seems to be sold on this one guy, Rev. W.L. Walker. Malcolm likes his preaching. He keeps you awake, and he talks about things that people are dealing with every day.

All the ladies like him, and I think they holler Amen because he's single, Malcolm thinks to himself. As he and Mama are walking out after church he looks over and sees a group of women, "I haven't seen those three women in a couple of years," he mumbles. He knows better than to say that aloud. Malcolm also notices that every Sunday the new preacher holds onto Mama's hand a little too long when they go by and shake hands after church. At first, he thinks it is because Mama found her voice. The church choir was doing this song a couple of weeks ago when the song leader starts coughing. All of a sudden, Shirley Wilson starts singing the lead from out in the pews. When the song ends, Rev. Walker said, "I think the angels in Heaven are standing and applauding your singing of God's word in song." On that Sunday, Shirley found her voice. She was not able to sing in public since Malcolm's funeral. She wondered to herself why God chose to give it back on that particular day. The one thing she knew for sure is it felt good to open up and sing once again. The choir members wanted her to come back and so did her mother. Mother Wilson always felt that if she got her voice back she would be able to live and love again.

In listening to his grandparents talk, Malcolm hears that Rev. Walker had a wife who died in childbirth while he was in Vietnam. The baby only lived a couple of days afterwards.

Grandpa Echols says, "Well he's single, but he's a good speaker. Seems to be doing a lot of good things in the community too. He's responsible for the city fixing up the park for the kids. I hope he can find himself a wife. It's better for the preacher to be married."

Malcolm thinks to himself, be careful what you ask for, you might just get it. Malcolm, being wise beyond his 12 years of age, notices the eye contact between Rev. Walker and Mama. He seems to show up out of nowhere whenever they go out. Always laughing and talking with Sister Wilson.

If I were a kid, Malcolm thinks to himself, these two might be able to pull the wool over my eyes. But man, Mama is as bad as he is. I've got more game than these two.

After a couple of surprise home visits in which the reverend says that he is, "just paying visits to the members." Malcolm decides somebody had better speak up. "Rev. Walker, could I have a few words with you on the front porch?" Malcolm asks him.

Stunned by this invitation, Shirley and the Reverend sat there looking at Malcolm and each other. After getting his thoughts together, Rev. Walker responds, "Certainly Malcolm." Malcolm says to his mother, "This is just between us men."

Shirley sat there quietly with her mouth still hanging open not knowing exactly what to say. Us men, she thinks. He couldn't even reach the top of the refrigerator for bread this morning without a chair to stand on. "Yes sir son," came out all by itself.

Malcolm and Rev. Walker sat in the two rockers on the front porch with their ice tea. Malcolm, to his own surprise, realized he may be in a little over his head, cleared his throat.

"Reverend," he began, "as the man of this house I need to know exactly what are your intentions toward my mama. You see. I have to look out for her. She depends on me."

"Well, Malcolm," says Rev. Walker, "I would like for her to come to depend on us. You know it wouldn't hurt if she had two men in her life she could depend on." Malcolm likes his answer so he decides to let him talk. "Malcolm, I've been single ever since my wife and child died while I was overseas, and until I met your mother, marriage never crossed my mind. You know; my son would have been about your age now."

"Reverend, you're not looking for a replacement family are you?" Malcolm can't believe he asked that. He certainly does not mean to be disrespectful. "Sorry Rev. Walker, I didn't mean for that to come out that way."

"No offense taken son," says Rev. Walker, "I appreciate your honesty. No, I'm not trying to replace anyone. There can be no replacement for what has already gone. Malcolm, you know I hated the government for having me so far away when my wife and baby died. It showed up in my life, even after I accepted my call into the ministry. My pastor finally told me I would have to forgive the people who were over me. However, most important, forgive myself for being unable to do anything about the situation. When you learn to love, there is no room for hate. He told me I would be able to love again, but only when I was able to appreciate the blessings God was sending my way. Hate and love can never reside in the same house at the same time. But to learn to love again takes a long time."

Oh Lord, Malcolm thinks to himself, I hadn't planned on hearing the L word. This man has got it bad.

Rev. Walker asked Malcolm, "How would you feel about having me around full time?"

Whoa! Hold your horses, Malcolm thinks to himself. I hadn't planned on all this. "What are we talking about?" Malcolm asked.

"Malcolm," says Rev. Walker, "with your approval, I would like to ask your mother to marry me."

"Don't you need Papa Wilson's OK on this?" Malcolm asked

"Only if you and I can agree," says Rev. Walker. "You see, you and I have to agree to work together to make your mother happy, or else; it's a waste of time. Plus, there is one other thing," continues Rev. Walker. "If she says yes, I would like for you to take the Walker name. I would like to adopt you. Now that you know my terms what do you say?"

Malcolm stood up, shook Rev. Walker's hand and said, "Preacher let's go in the house so you can get busy asking for her hand."

"Malcolm, if she says yes, I'd like for you and Papa Wilson to walk her down the aisle when you give her away," says Rev. Walker.

Malcolm looks at him and smiles, "Reverend, I won't give her away; but I will share her with you."

At this point, the young boy and the man embraced. This was the start of a relationship that would fill a home with joy and laughter in the years to come. There would always be love and respect between these two men.

The wedding of Shirley Wilson and Rev. Walker was the social event of the year. The entire community came out to see the hometown girl marry the new preacher. Very few of the single female members were there. As the wedding march started to play, the doors of the church opened, there stood Shirley, Papa Wilson, and Malcolm. He stood ready to share the first lady of his life with Rev. Walker. As they took that first step together, Malcolm smiled and thought to himself, Rev. Walker loves Mama, and she deserves this day. We agreed Rev. Walker is out, and Pops is in. Yea, I like that.

A new chapter in Malcolm's life has begun. Pops is there for all his ball games, PTA meetings, and he and Mama even chaperoned his Junior Prom. Just to look up in the stands to see

Pops rooting for him made him the proudest player on the team. One of Malcolm's proudest days was when he stood at the window of the hospital nursery to see his baby brother for the first time.

He had a good life with Mama, but he always wanted brothers and sisters like the other kids. Now, Richard Walker has made his entrance. Malcolm tells everybody they are going to call him Rick. He tells little Rick one day as he sat and held him in his arms. "Don't worry little brother, I'll teach you the ropes. That's what big brothers are for." Three years later, Miss Emily Walker made her grand entrance. Everything is complete now. He has a brother and sister now.

Talk about an over-protective big brother. When the time came for Malcolm to go off to college he wasn't sure he wanted to leave home. Who would be there to protect his little brother and sister? Pops and Mama assured him they were very capable of taking over for him.

Chapter 6

Life's Decisions

Choice of which college to attend came down to state institutions because they were the most affordable for Malcolm's family, and he chose Central State University. They accepted the first black students about ten years ago. So he will not feel out of place there. Plus, it's only about 50 miles away. He can still come home on the weekends to see Rick and Emily.

Thinking that his tuition is still stretching his parent's budget, Malcolm takes a job as a dispatcher for the campus police department. Pops and Mama told him he could keep the job as long as his grades stayed at a minimum of 3.0. He only has to work three evenings a week. The money helps out, but it causes him to cut his trips home on some weekends to see his family and attend church. But being raised in a preacher's house, all PKs know you go to church on Sundays, whether they are home or not. There is one a couple of blocks from the campus, The St. Paul Baptist Church.

    Each Sunday that Malcolm goes to church, he notices one girl who sits on the third pew. She is always with three other girls. He cannot tell you anything about the other three, but this one, he can describe her from head to toe. After church, people are always milling around, so it's hard to get a word with her. Plus, he has to go straight from church to work for the Sunday evening shift. One night during Malcolm's shift, it had been somewhat busy, and he had no time to stop for lunch. While on his way home, he stopped by the campus pizza house to get a couple of slices to take to his room. After he paid for his food and turned around, there sat that gorgeous female along with her three friends. Now was his chance to speak to her, and he couldn't say a word. As he stood there searching the universe for the right words to say, she spoke up and said, "Hi, aren't you Malcolm? I see you in church on Sundays when you make it."

How did she know that? Malcolm thought to himself. "Yes," was the only word that would come out. After all, he did remember his own name. This was the girl from church.

She introduces herself, "My name is Wanda, and these are my friends." Malcolm never heard their names. He had longed to meet her but never thought she had noticed him. He had dated a couple of girls in high school, but never had there been one to leave him speechless. Anyway, how did she know his name?

"Nice to meet you." Man that sounded dorky, Malcolm thinks to himself.

But Wanda never notices. She keeps right on talking. "My friends and I are having a late-night snack. Would you like to join us?"

"Well, I would," says Malcolm "but four beautiful women would be a little too much for me to handle this late."

"My dorm is right across the street," she tells him. "So, I guess I'll see you in church on Sunday."

Malcolm makes his way to his dorm. As he lay in bed unable to sleep, his roommate comes in, takes one look at him and says, "Roomy, you look like a man in love."

The days would not go by fast enough for Sunday to come. Malcolm asked the day dispatcher if he could give him one hour before he had to report in. That hour was all he needed to win her over.

Amen was really the only word Malcolm heard that Sunday. That meant services were over, and he could actually have a conversation with Wanda. He wondered why he hadn't seen her on campus. It turns out, she is an education major and they were on the opposite sides of the campus. That large campus just got a lot smaller.

This was one of the greatest days of his life. From this day forward, he would make many trips across campus to see Wanda.

As it turns out, she had seen him on campus and in church and had asked around to find out who he was.

Not too many young guys on campus were able to find their way to church all by themselves, Malcolm was a rare commodity. Some of the other girls had mentioned him, but thought he was a little too straight laced for them. But, not for Wanda.

It was understood in his home that you go to college to get an education, not to chase girls. Those were Pop's words. Plus he had to set an example for the younger ones. As the oldest child in the family, he set the tone, and this was the code that Malcolm lived by. He wasn't going to let Wanda knock him off track, but she has certainly become a big part of his plans for the future. This was what Pops meant when he said, "You'll know when you meet the right one."

During his junior year of college, Malcolm makes a decision that stunned the entire family and Wanda. He first tells Wanda of his decision to join the Centerville Police Department. He asked Wanda to go home with him that weekend to break the news. Maybe when Pops and Mama meet Wanda they'll be too stunned to give him a hard time about college he reasons. To his dismay, they love her and they all gang up on him for wanting to drop out of school. He doesn't want to drop out, once he joins the force; he will utilize the Law Enforcement Educational Program the force has that will pay for his college. Malcolm tells them, "That way, my job will pay for school and you guys will be off the hook."

After a long discussion, they finally reach an agreement. Take the job as long as you promise to complete your education. Wanda chimes in she will stop dating him if he doesn't have his degree by the time she gets hers.

On their way back to school Malcolm asked Wanda, "Did you mean what you told my folks?"

"Sure did," she replied, "we have to set a good example for our children in the future."

That was all Malcolm Walker needed to hear. Depending on when he got into the police academy, he may only have to lay out one semester of college.

Fresh from recruiting class number 42, Officer Malcolm Walker hits the ground running. And so far, all of his reviews have been great. There seems to be a defining moment in every officer's life, and Malcolm's moment came about 4:00 p.m. on a Thursday evening. A bank robbery call came over the air with all available officers responding. A standoff developed when the police got there before the culprit could get out of the bank. The bank robber was holding bank employees and customers as hostages.

With everyone waiting for a supervisor to arrive on the scene, Officer Walker took the initiative and made use of some training from the Negotiators School handbook he had been reading. He made contact with the bank robber inside the bank. When the supervisor, Lieutenant Hanger, arrived on the scene,

Malcolm had all the hostages released and the robber backing out of the bank with his hands in the air. When Lieutenant Hanger asked, "who was responsible for this?" Everybody pointed to Walker. The comment was made, "He's a good one Lieutenant, and we need to keep him."

Hanger asked him, "Son, how did you learn to do that so quickly?"

Malcolm replied, "Well sir, the information I was reading in Negotiator's School handbook came in really handy. Plus, my Pops is our pastor back home. I have listened to him every Sunday for years. He can probably convince the devil to give up his pitchfork. I just told that guy some of the things I've heard him preach about. He made the decision to give up."

Lieutenant Hanger shakes his hand on a job well done. At the same time, he's thinking there is something special about this kid. However, he couldn't put his finger on it, but what does stand out is that this kid has the same first name as the friend who saved his life –Malcolm. He then thinks about the incident that led him to consider law enforcement. As he prepares to clear the scene, he can only think, now that is the way it is supposed to be done.

The next day as Malcolm is walking across campus headed for class, Wanda walks up, kisses him on the cheek and asked, "Well, how is my little hero today?" When he finally convinces her he doesn't know what she is talking about, she shows him the morning newspaper. The headline reads "Robber Talked Out by Police." On the trip home that following weekend, the entire church congregation applauds Malcolm. As he and Wanda take their seat next to Mama, there are Rick and Emily seated next to them. They are not just sitting with the local hero of the day; they're sitting with their big brother, who is the greatest police officer in the world.

Malcolm's climb within the department has been rapid. He is a real shining star, but not without some distractions. There are those who feel Chief Hanger favors him too much. When there were two coveted spots in the Negotiator's School, he was an automatic shoe in for the first one. The Chief's son, Paul, was finally able to land the other.

Malcolm and Paul are good friends, and there is a great deal of respect between the two. However, Paul feels he has to compete with Malcolm for Chief Hanger's attention on the job.

There is no real reason for him to be intimidated. Malcolm and his family have been a part of their lives ever since he was a young boy. He has heard all about how Malcolm talked a bank robber into giving up and admires his skills. For a man he knows and admires so much, Paul really does not understand why he feels the need to compete with him.

Malcolm's ascent up through the ranks was well noted within the department. He was the youngest officer to ever be promoted to the rank of Sergeant. Some of the old timers have problems taking orders from a young black guy. Chief Hanger wanted to step in but Malcolm asked him not to.

One day after working the 3 to 11 shift, Malcolm encountered a peculiar situation. After clocking out for the night, Malcolm noticed some officers standing on the steps of the academy building. As he headed toward his car, he spoke to them. At his car, he unlocked the door, stepped in, and put the key in the ignition. When he turned the key, a loud popping sound could be heard. It sounded like a shot from a pistol.

Malcolm rolled out of the car onto the ground with his weapon drawn. It was then that smoke starting rising from under the hood of his car. He holstered his weapon and raised the hood. A cherry bomb had been placed on the coil. When the ignition fired, the cherry bomb exploded. The guys standing on the steps were laughing so hard they couldn't stand up straight.

Malcolm walked over to them and said, "Guys; we need to talk. I love a good joke just as much as the next guy, but you have gone too far. You are messing with my money. I have to pay for that car, and that's no joke. So, you had better understand this. If either of you ever touch anything else I own, I'm going to find you, and if I have to, shoot you right on the spot. In fact, you're the same ones who are always using the word nigger on the radio. That is going to stop also. As a group, you sound tough, but tonight why don't we find out what you're made of one by one."

At that point, Malcolm unhooks his gun belt and drops it. He takes off his badge and lays it down. He looks at them and asked, "Who's first?" No one moves. He stands there for what feels like an eternity, but it was only a few seconds. He then picks up his badge and pins it back on, picks up his gun belt and puts it back on. Then he tells them some words he will never forget and hopes they won't either.

"Gentleman," he says, "I know you don't love me. I really don't care if you don't even like me. But understand this, you're going to respect me." With that said Malcolm turns and walks back to his car, gets in and drives off into the night. The events of that night stretched beyond that night. He was able to deal with those guys in such a way that they now are some of his biggest supporters.

Supervising and training officers were two areas in which he could really shine. The crime rate went down in every district he was assigned. He always gave his officers the credit for the drop, and he would stand up for them.

Once he moved over to the detective department, he was able to clear open cases at a fantastic rate. Clearing cases and securing confessions were two areas in which he was able to excel.

Paul loves him, he admires him, and at the same time still feels a need to compete with him. As he sees Malcolm's status about to rise a bit higher, he makes a decision that will end the competition, at least in his mind anyway. His real desire is for his dad to look at him without seeing Malcolm's shadow.

Chapter 7

News from the Past

Here it is July 22, 2006, almost twenty years to the day that I joined the force; Malcolm thinks to himself. When I joined, I just wanted to be a beat cop and finish up my degree. Now today I'll be receiving my Lieutenant Gold Shield, Lieutenant Malcolm Walker, Chief of Detectives. That has a sweet ring to it. Without Chief Hanger's guidance, I don't know if I could have made it this far.

Wanda is taking the day off, and the kids will only miss a half day at school. It's important and, I want them to be proud of their old man. Growing up as a cop's kid had not been all bad.

Malcolm is lying in the bed. He can't wait for the alarm to go off, so he gets up and heads into the kitchen to make coffee. Later while standing in the mirror shaving, Wanda opens the door, hands him his cup of coffee and says, "Good morning Lieutenant, too excited to sleep." He smiles sheepishly.

As they prepare for what is truly a special day Wanda tells him not to worry. She knows how to get two teenagers up and moving. They will be there in plenty of time for the promotion ceremony. "Honey, be sure to call Mama and Rev. Walker so you can tell them where to park," she reminds him.

A light breakfast is all he can handle. He's too excited about today's events. As he heads out the door, he kisses Wanda and tells her he will see them at the station in a couple of hours. He can't help but think to himself that meeting her was one of the best things that ever happened to him.

"Call your mother," she reminds him as he walks out the door. Malcolm stopped right at the garage, opens his cell, scrolls down to Mama, and pushes send. On the second ring, a man answers. "Hey Pops," Malcolm says, "Will I see you today?"

"Son, wild horses couldn't keep us away. Boy, your mama raised you right, and we are proud of you. We love you son, now get off my phone."

They both laugh and hang up. Malcolm thinks to himself, that his pops is a good man as he backs out and heads for the station.

As he walks into the squad room, he's greeted with smiles and handshakes. "Morning Louie," one detective greets him.

"Hey, show some respect," Malcolm replied, "after all I am your boss." As he is taking off his coat, one of the guys brings him a cup of coffee. Instead of the regular Styrofoam cup, this one is a blue mug with Lieutenant Walker on it.

"Congrats, Malcolm, you deserve it," he says.

"Thanks man," says Malcolm, "now quit trying to kiss up. I haven't been promoted yet."

Malcolm settles in and takes a few calls. Some business, but most are calls of congratulations. Not only is he going to be the Chief of Detectives, but he also is the first black officer to hold this position. He understands what this means for the department. But, it means a great deal more for his community.

Malcolm prays quietly to himself, "Lord, make me worthy I'll be responsible for assigning the right people to the right cases to make sure every citizen is treated fairly. But, Lord I need you to watch my back. Mama always says you are everywhere. So, I really need you to walk with me. Amen"

The ringing of his phone breaks his concentration. His new secretary tells him. "Lieutenant, it's Chief Hanger on line one."

"Morning Chief," says Malcolm as he picks up the phone.

"Morning Lieutenant, could you come up to my office for a few minutes," says Chief Hanger.

"On my way Chief," Malcolm grabs his coat and heads upstairs. As he steps off the elevator, he was met by more congratulations. When he steps through the door, Chief Hanger is standing there.

"Lieutenant, step into my office," says Chief Hanger. As Malcolm goes in Chief Hanger closes the door. Malcolm, you've proven yourself," says Chief Hanger, "you are the right man for the job. Since we are not a huge department, our command staff is rather small. The Chief of Detectives is my right-hand man and second in command of the department. As we grow in size, your title will become Deputy Chief. We are not there yet, but we're headed that way. The city council will have to sign off on my reorganization structure. The city is growing, and we have to grow with it. Are you ready for a few personnel problems and city council meetings?"

"Yes Sir, I'll do my best,"" says Malcolm.

"Always giving your best is what got you here. I hate people who start making statements about why you're being promoted to this position," the Chief adds.

Malcolm says, "Chief, if there's one thing I do know, it's that you don't hate anybody. It's my job to prove the naysayers wrong by giving my best."

"You sound like my wife," says Hanger, "Have you guys been talking?"

Malcolm says, "Nope, but I think she knows you pretty well."

"Come on Malcolm," says Chief Hanger, "let's head downstairs. I'm really looking forward to seeing that beautiful wife of yours and my God Kids. Oh yea, will Reverend and Mrs. Walker make it?"

Malcolm said he spoke with Pops earlier. "In his words, wild horses couldn't keep them away."

"Great!" says the Chief. "Now let's get going. We wouldn't want everybody to beat you to your own promotion ceremony."

Once everyone had arrived, Malcolm's swearing in took place and pictures were taken by the local paper. The Mayor and some city council people were in attendance. It's a good day. While Malcolm, Pops, and the kids are shaking hands and taking pictures, Chief Hanger notices Mrs. Walker just sitting there and watching all the activities. She's very proud of Malcolm. He has always been a good boy and a great role model for the younger ones.

Chief Hanger goes over, takes the seat beside her, and tells her, "You know Mrs. Walker, you and Rev. Walker raised one fine man, and we are proud to have him with our department. We could be looking at my replacement when I decide to hang it up."

"Thank you Chief," Shirley Walker says, "but you know Rev. Walker adopted Malcolm when we married. He was twelve years old then, and I thank God the right man came into both our lives. Rev. Walker wanted all our kids to have the same last name. He and Malcolm worked that out between the two of them."

"Malcolm's real father died in Vietnam. His family received his medals and a letter from his commanding officer about his bravery on the battlefield. When his personal artifacts were returned, the letter I had written him to let him know I was pregnant came with them. It had been opened and had bloodstains on it. So, I hope he had gotten to read it before he died. I have all those items stored away so Malcolm can go through and learn about his dad whenever he wants. He and Rev. Walker went through them when he was a teenager. He was able to explain to Malcolm each of the medals and ribbons. Charles was able to help him understand just how great of a hero his dad really was. Being a veteran himself, he was better equipped to explain it to him than I could. Once those questions were answered in his mind there just hadn't been a lot of conversations about it. He has never asked for those items. I think he somehow knows they still hold some memories for me."

The Chief looks as though he has seen a ghost by now. Hardly able to get the words out, he asked the question. "What was his dad's name?"

Shirley looked at Chief Hanger and softly patted him on the arm as she said, "Sergeant Malcolm Echols." Now with tears in his eyes he can hardly speak, and he tries to say something. Shirley continues on, "You don't have to say a word Lieutenant

Thomas J. Hanger." It's funny how God works. The man whose life my Malcolm saved is the same man who has guided his son's career."

Chief Hanger is speechless. He can only ask the question, "How long have you known?"

Shirley says, "Well, his folks gave me his medal and letter of commendation from the Army. They knew his son would one day want to know about his father. You see I know he didn't leave me. God took him because he was ready. Later, I requested information from the Army about how he died. The information I received referred to a Lieutenant Thomas J. Hanger. It was easy to put two and two together."

"Does Malcolm know," Chief Hanger asked, "that I'm the reason he grew up without a father? If he had looked out for himself instead of me, he probably would be alive today."

"Chief," Shirley tells him, "if Malcolm had done anything other than what he did to save you, he would not have been the man I fell in love with all those years ago. Putting others before himself came natural for him. My son was already under your wing when I found out. Rev. Walker and I agreed that one day, when the time was right, that maybe you should be the one to tell him. You're probably the best one suited to tell him about Sergeant Malcolm Echols. I think if it comes from you, that will make him even prouder of his dad. After all, what boy doesn't want a hero for a father?"

The Chief can only say, "Thank you" at this point. He thinks to himself; I always wondered how I would be able to repay the debt I owed Sergeant Malcolm Echols. I had no idea the young man I took under my wing was his son. Fate is a strange thing. God places people in your life for you to love and doesn't really tell you why."

"What are you two plotting about over here?" Malcolm asks as he walks up.

"Oh, just talking about a great man," Shirley replied.

He gives her a kiss on the cheek and goes back to the others. Chief Hanger asked Shirley. "Is it true that angels in Heaven stand and clap when you sing?"

Shirley smiled and replied, "I've never heard them myself, but thank you for remembering. That means an awful lot to me."

Chapter 8

Love is an Action Word

As Thomas Hanger has watched Malcolm progress and grow as an officer, he has done everything he can to assist his career. Over the years, he and Malcolm have grown close on a personal basis. He was there for Malcolm and Wanda's wedding. When their kids were born, he was there to keep Malcolm from walking a hole in the carpet and to welcome them into the world. He and Helen are the kids' God Parents.

However, Hanger's career progressed as well. He has climbed the ranks and was considered by all as the one person responsible for bringing the department into the 21st century. The nameplate on his desk now reads Chief Thomas J. Hanger.

In his personal life, he has faired well too. His son has grown into a fine young man. He's considered by Paul as his hero. When Paul was in school, his mom and dad were always right there sitting in the stands rooting for him at all of his football and baseball games. After every touchdown he scored, Paul would always give a special wave to his dad. In return, Hanger would give that special wave back. This was their special communication between father and son.

Following high school, Paul went to Central State University. It was his choice. He could have gone to any school he chose, but Central was right here in town and was his folk's alma mater. After all, there was a tradition he had to keep up.

Upon graduation, Paul felt it was only natural for him to follow in his dad's footsteps. So, he joined the Centerville Police Department. But he was only allowed to call Chief Hanger dad at home. Sometimes he would call him Chief at the house as a joke.

On a quiet evening when they were both off duty, Paul finally tells his dad of his aspirations to move to a different level of law enforcement. He had applied for the FBI. He wanted to become Special Agent Paul Hanger.

Chief Hanger could not tell him he had already received calls from an agent he had worked with over the years. They were letting him know how happy they were to bring Paul on board. He's proud of his son and wanted to hear the news from him.

Paul was afraid his dad's feelings were going to be hurt over him wanting to leave the department. Thomas assures him the only feelings he has were those of pride. In less than thirty days, Paul would be leaving the department for the FBI Academy.

On the day of the promotion ceremony, Paul was at the Police Academy training the recruit class on how to disarm subjects. He tells the other trainer to take his weapon and let him be the bad guy for a change. As the demonstration moves forward, the weapon is drawn and the trigger pulled.

"BANG!!"

To their shock and dismay, a round goes off.

The Sergeant over training hears the shot and goes running down the hallway to see what has happened. As he rounds the corner, he sees Paul Hanger on the floor holding his stomach. Kyle Jenkins is on his knees beside him holding his head telling him to hold on. Kyle has a phone in the other hand calling 911, telling them to get there quick, an officer has been shot. Those rookies in the training session are standing around not knowing what to do. The Sergeant calls for some towels. He keeps pressure on the wound and keeps talking to Paul. They don't want him to lose consciousness.

Once the ambulance arrives, the paramedics begin to treat Paul. They get him stabilized and loaded into the ambulance for transport. Kyle wants to go with Paul but knows he can't. He has to stay and explain what and how everything happened. The Supervising Sergeant advised the trainees to sit down and write in their own words what they saw happen. Kyle knows to leave the gun on the floor and not touch anything.

Things are not moving fast enough for Kyle. He needs to get to the hospital to see about his friend. Paul was the reason he decided to join the police force in the first place. They have been best friends since junior high school. They did everything together, and he was a constant fixture in the Hanger house. They were like his second family.

His dad took off when he was a kid. His mom did the best she could raising him, but when he needed a man to talk with, Thomas Hanger was there for him. The Hanger family took him everywhere they went. Whether it was for ice cream, camping, or on a family vacation, it was always Paul and Kyle. Now he has done something to hurt the ones he loves the most. He can only think, Chief Hanger was going to hate him for this.

"Hey, you've got to hurry up. I've got to get to the hospital," he shouts to the officers coming in to investigate.

After the ceremony and while Chief Hanger and Lieutenant Walker were still enjoying the events of the day, it seemed as though every telephone in the room started ringing all at once. Information on a shooting started coming in. As he starts up to his office, Chief of Detectives Walker stops Chief Hanger. The call Malcolm received was to inform him of the officer's name who had been shot.

"Chief," Malcolm tells him, "the wounded officer is Paul. He's stable and on his way to the hospital."

"I'll send some guys over to investigate," says Malcolm, "but right now let's get you over to the hospital."

"Let's hurry," says Chief Hanger. "His mother is on duty, and I don't want her seeing him like that." Many thoughts run through Chief Hanger's mind. Thomas was proud of Paul; he was proud of everything from his first steps to the day Paul graduated from the academy.

He tells Malcolm, "Whoever is responsible for this, I'll hate them until the day I die."

They get to the hospital seconds after the ambulance carrying Paul arrives. Helen has been made aware something bad has happened. She is now in the emergency room with Hanger and

Walker. The phones are still ringing off the hook. The news media has picked up word of the shooting incident. Radio and television reporters arrive at the hospital, and it's Malcolm's job to deal with them. He will only tell them an officer was injured in a training accident, and the extent of his injury according to the doctors. Everybody is seeking information about the shooting. The word is the same for all. No name was given because they wanted to be sure the family is notified first.

Chief Hanger says," Malcolm, you know we're already here."

"That's right," replies Malcolm, "but that will keep them off your doorstep for a little while. You and Helen have enough on your plates at the moment. I'll give them the names of all involved when the time is right. Right now, I need more information so I can decide what to give out. Paul is in surgery, and we're waiting."

Malcolm receives a call from one of his detectives giving him details of how the shooting took place. He hangs up, and he and the Chief step out of the room. Standing there in the hallway, he gives Chief Hanger the details of how the incident went down and who the other officer was.

Paul went to the academy to assist Kyle with that portion of the training as he always does. He was on the phone when he walked in. Before he entered the room, he dropped the clip, but forgot to clear the chamber before he holstered his weapon. When he stepped in, he handed Jenkins the weapon. Jenkins assumed it had been cleared. It would have been Jenkins on the other end of that weapon if Paul hadn't decided to switch roles at the last minute.

Chief of Detectives Walker has decided the only name that will be released to the public is that of the injured officer, and that can wait until after he is out of surgery. All others will be held pending the completion of the investigation.

Hanger can't believe his ears. Paul handed the gun to the other officer without clearing it first. About this time, Officer Kyle Jenkins rounds the corner. Through his tears, he tells Hanger, "Chief, I know you hate me for what happened, and you have every right to. I'm sorry, I don't know what else to say. Paul gave me the weapon, but I should have double-checked it."

Chief Hanger stops him, "Kyle, I don't hate you son. You and Paul have been the best of friends since junior high school. If there was one person he trusted, it's you. I've already been brought up to speed on how this happened. Regardless to the outcome today, I could never hate you. You've been like a son to us."

"Can you and Mrs. Hanger ever forgive me?" Kyle asked.

"There's nothing to forgive," says Chief Hanger, "we still love you."

As they sit and wait, Hanger tells Malcolm, "I need to speak with you in private."

They excuse themselves from Mrs. Hanger, Wanda, and the others who have come to support them. As these two men sit off to themselves, Hanger tells Malcolm the story of how his father, Sergeant Malcolm Echols, saved his life. He tells him of how he initially felt about black people, but came to respect him and love him as a friend. He explains how he had no idea of this connection until today when Shirley told him everything.

"Malcolm, I hope you can forgive me. I'm the one responsible for his death," says Hanger.

"No Chief, you're not responsible," says Malcolm, "my dad gave his life saving a friend and brother in arms. I thank God it was you he saved. I guess in a way he knew I would need you down the line."

About this time the doctor comes out, "We were able to save him, and we have got him stable," says the doctor, "but he's going to need a blood transfusion if he's going to make it to tomorrow. His blood type is rare, AB Negative, and they are putting out a call all over the county.

Right then Malcolm speaks up, "That's my blood type: no need to look any further."

Hanger can't believe his ears. "You're willing to save my son after what I just told you?"

"He's my brother in arms," says Malcolm, "that's what my dad would want me to do."

With those words, Malcolm Echols Walker went down the hallway with the doctor, going to save another life. Just like his dad had done.

Chief Hanger stands there so totally mystified by all that is going on around him. One man has come to him asking for forgiveness when none was needed. The other has volunteered to save his son's life out of love when he could have hate in his heart. He stands there realizing there is just no one left to hate.

Chapter 9

A Tested Friendship

Malcolm started coming around the Hanger household when Paul was just a kid. Paul enjoyed sitting and listening to his dad and Malcolm talk shop about police work, and the best way to handle different situations. Chief Hanger would then instruct Malcolm to consider different viewpoints in those situations. Maybe part of Paul's desire to follow in his dad's footsteps was born out of hearing the excitement in their voices as they talked about the best way to handle them. He knew his dad had a great deal of respect for this college kid who decided he wanted to be a police officer.

It had been about three months since the accidental shooting where Paul was severely wounded. He had a really nice bachelor pad all laid out exactly as he wanted. A young woman he was dating at the time helped him to decorate it. But, at his mother's insistence, when he was released from the hospital, he went back home to live with his parents so Helen could nurse him back to health. She told him she could take better care of him at home rather than running back and forth across town. Helen had taken leave from the hospital, so she could be there for her son.

Malcolm had called the day before to see if Paul was ready for company. As he walked in, Helen told him out of all the guys who had come by to see Paul there was some excitement in his voice when she said Malcolm was coming over.

As Malcolm walked into the den, Paul greeted him with a hug as he said thank you again and again. The two men went out to the patio where they could sit and talk. This is also the spot where Malcolm and Chief Hanger had spent many hours in deep conversation. Paul said, "Dad told me everything. He told me the story about him and your real dad. He told me of how he was willing to give his life to keep a promise. Only to find out right before he died, he was going to be a father also. I feel there is a debt I owe him, because he allowed me to grow up with my dad.

Dad says he had always wondered how he would ever be able to repay that type of debt, only to realize no payment is enough for some debts."

When the veteran police officer met this young rookie, that repayment was not on his mind. He could only see another police officer who did things the way he believed they should be done. Paul remembered hearing his dad tell his mom this young kid is a true natural. His people skills are the best I have ever seen in any police officer. Paul recalled hearing his dad say, "I really like this kid. There's no telling how far he can go."

Paul also remembers Malcolm coming to his football games and cheering him on. He was always happy to see him, and the two of them would often talk about many different things. In fact, there were things they would talk about when Paul didn't feel comfortable going to his mom or dad. Malcolm had one steadfast rule. If it was something he felt was too sensitive and he thought it was more on the level of what a son should talk to his dad about, he would say "Paul I can't answer that question, you need to talk with your dad about this one."

Whenever he went to his dad with one of those questions it would always start out, "Dad, Malcolm told me I should come to you with this one." The Hangers appreciated Malcolm being a sort of big brother to Paul and knew he would never lead him astray.

Paul tells Malcolm that if it had not been for him coming to the rescue, he might not have made it. Paul has been asking himself, "How do you repay someone who saves your life?" Thank you doesn't seem to be good enough. However, that's all he can think to say so he tells Malcolm again, "Thank you."

Those two words are more than sufficient for Malcolm. Malcolm tells him, "You were always going to make it. It was a blessing for me to be the one there at that moment to give you the transfusion. Maybe this makes us more like blood brothers now." That comment evoked a roar of laughter between the two of them that brought tears to both their eyes.

As the conversation dwindles down to a quiet moment, Paul tells Malcolm he knew he was his friend. "I guess I took it for granted that you would always be there. Our lives have been intertwined with the law enforcement careers and their personal lives. Even your wedding was a big deal in our home. The Hanger family was proud to sit with the Walkers that day." Paul even made a trip to the maternity ward when Malcolm's son was born. Paul talked with Malcolm before he approached his folks about joining the police department.

He admits that once he got on the department and started trying to get into different specialized schools, he thought being the Chief's son would get him some preferential treatment. His dad, the Chief, had warned him against trying to use that connection. Paul always took everything his dad said to heart, but in the back of his mind he did hope that connection would pay off a little, but, it seemed that if anybody had a leg up, it was Malcolm. "Somehow you became the competition. If there were only two openings, one was automatically yours, and I had to fight with everyone for the other," said Paul. "I know that is not the way it was, but it felt that way at the time," Paul admits. "I allowed some voices who were not fans of yours to get in my head and for a moment there, I got a little jealous. The time spent together, and the trust of a friend; it all seemed so distant at the time. The man who had been my friend was turning into my competition. But, it was not you who brought this attitude about, rather my feelings that I had to compete with you for my dad's approval on the job. So, I started distancing myself from you. There were plenty of talking heads out there who were telling me I was right. I didn't just want to be like you, I wanted to be better than you. Everything I did had to top you. I wanted people to start calling my name as the top cop on the department. You were just simply doing your best, and I'm not sure what I wanted.

    I know dad was proud when I decided to follow in his footsteps. But to see how he felt about the things you were accomplishing, made me somewhat jealous. You became my competition for the pats on the back from the man I most admired, my own father. Once I started to realize the problem wasn't you, I knew a change needed to be made. It was at that point I started looking at becoming my own man where I didn't need the approval of my dad. After a lot of soul searching, I made the decision to apply to the F.B.I. There I wouldn't be the Chief's son or your competition, but my own man. There I can do what he has always taught me to do, stand on my own two feet."

"Where do things stand now?" Malcolm asked. "I notified the people at Quantico as soon as I felt good enough to talk on the phone. In addition, I've been in contact with the agent here who was processing my paperwork. Once the doctors clear me, I will have to undergo an extra tough physical before they clear me for the academy. There is a class starting in about six months. The doctors tell me I'll be more than ready by then." Paul tells Malcolm, "Dad told me the story about your father and how if it had not been for him, there's a good chance, he would not have survived Vietnam. He put himself in harm's way to save a man he had only known for less than a year. He always wondered how he could repay a debt of that magnitude. When you came along, he says that debt was the last thing on his mind. But, what he saw was a young man who was a natural at this job. He was impressed that you wanted to serve the people and regardless of the situation, everyone deserved to be treated with dignity and respect."

Malcolm tells Paul of how much his folks were against him becoming a police officer. "My Pops told me I did not have to worry about paying for college. He could easily afford to pay for my education. After we talked, I had to promise to go back to college and finish my education. However, this was something I felt called to do. God has a place for each one of us in this world. We just have to listen to what it is he's telling us. I knew I didn't have to get a job, but I felt it was something he was leading me to do. They even said wait until after graduation and if that was what

I still wanted to do they would support my decision. I wouldn't try to convince my son to follow in my footsteps. I want him to follow the path God has laid out for him, and I will support him in his decisions."

Paul asked," How did you feel when you found out your father died saving my dad?"

"Well I was somewhat shocked," says Malcolm. "Chief Hanger had just found out about the connection a couple of hours before he pulled me aside. So I think he was still trying to process the information in his mind while he was telling me the story. I think he wondered how this would cause me to feel toward him. He didn't take me under his wing because he felt sorry for me or felt he owed me something. He gave me that extra hand because he felt I could become even a better officer. In case you didn't know it, I'm not the only one he has reached out to help. Some of us accepted that hand, and others didn't have enough sense too. He wants all of his officers to be the best they can be. Neither of us had any idea of the connection between he and my father. I'm really glad it happened that way, If things hadn't worked out with me, then he may have felt he had let his friend down. God may have taken my father through a sacrificial act for his fellow man. He gave me two good men in his place.

When Pops, Rev. Walker, came into our lives, God was not substituting or replacing the family he had lost years earlier. He was putting people in the lives of each other who had love to give and a life to share with each other. Pops had so much love to give and my mom and I were the ones God placed in his life when he was ready to share it. I had both of my grandfathers, so I wasn't missing any male role models. I needed him in my life to help me grow into a man.

What your dad told me was he saw a young officer who had a lot of potential. God placed him in my life to help me grow. We formed a bond that even I can't explain today. But I can tell you that what he did for me made a world of difference in my life.

That's really what it is all about. We are here in this world to be a blessing to each other. That's what your dad has done for me. Getting to know you and your mother was a real plus in my life. I could spend the rest of my life wondering what I missed by not knowing my real dad. I could be mad at God for what some may say was taken away from me, but look at what God has done for me by placing two great men in my life to help me grow and prosper. So rather than being mad, I'm thankful. I don't look at what I lost, but rather what I gained. So how can I be upset? At least for me, getting to know the man my dad saved turned out to be such a great person really does make a difference. Do I wish I had gotten to know my dad? Yea I do, that's something I will always wish had happened. However, that's not the way God chose to do things. As much as I've wanted to question him about the way things happened, I've been taught, and I understand what the scriptures say, *God's ways are not our ways, his thoughts are not our thoughts.* God is still in control, and I think he's done a pretty good job by me. I really hadn't missed a thing. Between my grandfathers, Pops, and Chief Hanger, I would say I'm very blessed."

"Our friendship," Malcolm continues, "is one that is very special to me. Even the best relationships hit a rough spot here and there."

"I hope ours is on smooth ground now," Paul responds. "Oh yea, it's taken some maturing on my part to really understand what it means to have a true friend. I hope you can forgive me for the way I've acted."

"No apology necessary," says Malcolm, "you're my friend, plus you know this means we are blood brothers now." They both laugh aloud over that one. "But, we're really going to have to work on Kyle. He really thinks somebody should hate him for what happened, and it's weighing heavily on his mind. He feels he hurt his best friend."

Paul says, "It was an accident, and I was more at fault than anyone because I failed to follow the proper procedure. He just happened to be the one on the other end of the gun."

As they talked about what they needed to do to help a friend neither of them was aware that Helen Hanger was sitting in the den and could hear their conversation. She was so pleased to hear the boy she raised had grown into a real man and the young man who has come to be such an important figure of their lives were once again on solid ground. Malcolm had shown just how much Paul meant to him when he told the doctors he would give the blood for the transfusion Paul needed. Now Paul understands what it means to have a true friend. Even though the decision to go to the F.B.I. is one Paul feels he needs to stick with, there is a bond between these two men that has been solidified through more than the average person can understand.

Just as they were wrapping up their talk, Chief Hanger comes in from work. Helen tells him of the conversation she has just overheard. Charles then makes a very profound statement, "We love Kyle, and he thinks we should hate him. Malcolm has every reason to hate, but he chooses to love us instead. You know, there is No One Left to Hate."

We often see things happen in our lives and in the lives of others and call them coincidences, but all the time it is God's hand moving in our lives.

CPSIA information can be obtained
at www.ICGtesting.com
Printed in the USA
FFOW05n1115240214